Jo grew up in North London, where she met her husband and later they moved to Dorset.

She has worked with young children in nurseries and pre-schools and holds qualifications in Montessori education and childcare.

She now works as a qualified holistic and beauty therapist and finds her work very rewarding. She has three children and four grandchildren whom she likes to spend time with. Writing for children is something she has always been interested in and a holiday last year gave her the opportunity to make a start.

PEARL ISLAND

Josephine Barker

AUSTIN MACAULEY PUBLISHERS™
LONDON • CAMBRIDGE • NEW YORK • SHARJAH

A CIP catalogue record for this title is available from the British Library.

ISBN 9781528915311 (Paperback)
ISBN 9781528961196 (ePub e-book)

www.austinmacauley.com

First Published (2019)
Austin Macauley Publishers Ltd
25 Canada Square
Canary Wharf
London
E14 5LQ

For all my grandchildren, whom I love dearly.

To my husband. Thank you for being my paper-runner.

When the children awoke, they were already there. Abbie pulled the curtains back and the sun shone through the window, lighting the children's bunks and filling the room with dazzling sunlight.

Through the window, they could see the sea, it was the most beautiful turquoise you could imagine.

'Wow, we're here, everyone, we're here,' Abbie yelled in excitement.

The children were so excited to be on holiday, having just finished school several days previously.

This year, Nanny and Grandad were taking them to Pearl Island, a small island in the Atlantic Ocean.

'I can't believe we're on this yacht,' said Jack, 'we're so lucky that Grandad's friend let us use it – and for a whole fortnight.'

'Two weeks, Jack, not a fortnight. Whatever that is!' exclaimed Lola mockingly and feeling rather important now that Jack didn't know what he was talking about.

'A fortnight is two weeks, you wally,' laughed Jack, turning and pulling a face at Lola.

'Come on,' said Abbie, 'let's get up and go and see what's upstairs.'

The children leapt out of bed and, in no time at all, had thrown on their dressing gowns and slippers and scrambled upstairs to the upper deck.

Nanny and Grandad were already up and having breakfast.

'Well, well,' laughed Nanny. 'Here you are at last. We wondered when you were going to wake up, sleepy heads.'

'Is this Pearl Island?' asked Abbie. 'Are we here?'

'Yes, we're here,' replied Grandad.

'Hurray!' the children cried and they danced around the deck, squirming and squealing with excitement.

Bella was only two and didn't really understand what all the excitement was about, but she was happy to join in and run around in circles, copying the other children.

'Right,' said Nanny, 'before you do anything else today, you will need a good breakfast inside you.'

After breakfast, Abbie and Jack explored the yacht while Bella and Lola played with their dolls on deck.

The yacht had a dinghy so the family could leave and visit neighbouring beaches or go fishing.

Abbie had attended lessons in sailing and was an experienced sailor, even for her young years.

Seb, the captain of the yacht, and Grandad had agreed that Abbie and Jack could take the dinghy out on their own, but only after they had been out with Seb. They were to spend the first week practising and getting used to the conditions.

Jack and Abbie were excited. Today, they were going to take the dinghy out on their own. Lowering the dinghy into the water, they carefully climbed in. They headed towards the headland to the left side of the cove.

The rocky headland was craggy with sparse green shrubs and windswept pine trees clinging to the rock's surface. On top of the cliff were the remains of an ancient castle where seagulls glided above.

Towards the end of the headland, there was a tiny cave, no bigger than a doorway. The children hadn't noticed this before but, as they got nearer, they could see a tiny light glowing deep inside.

'What do you think that is, Jack?' whispered Abbie slightly nervously.

'Don't know,' replied Jack, 'we'll get a bit nearer and see.'

Abbie guided the dinghy nearer to the entrance of the doorway cave.

The sea was calm, which made the dinghy easier to manoeuvre.

Abbie carefully steered the boat through the entrance with Jack pushing against the sides of the cave to help guide it through. It was a tight fit but they made it.

'Can you still see the light?' Jack asked Abbie.

'No, where's it gone?' she questioned.

'I know, I'll get my torch out. That will shine some light for us to see better,' Jack replied.

'Ahhh, who's that there?' gasped a grouchy voice from the darkness.

'Oh no!' cried Abbie in alarm. 'There's someone there, Jack, I'm scared, let's go.'

'Hang on a minute, Abbie, let's see who it is,' Jack replied.

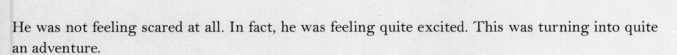

He was not feeling scared at all. In fact, he was feeling quite excited. This was turning into quite an adventure.

'Who's that there?' demanded Jack in his boldest voice.

'Err… I said it first,' replied the voice from the darkness, sounding slightly nervous now.

Jack and Abbie giggled. They thought this person was probably not as scary after all.

'Show yourself,' demanded Jack, feeling fully in control and shining the torch as far into the darkness as it would go.

Slowly, from behind a rock, a dirty bearded man appeared.

'I'm, I'm, I'm a pirate,' he stuttered, 'so you'd better watch yourselves.'

'A pirate!' exclaimed the children. 'Where's your hat and your pirate ship, then?' laughed Jack.

'Well, here's my hat,' the pirate replied, retrieving a dusty, frayed old hat from behind a rock.

He shook it before plonking it on his head, slightly skew-whiff.

The skull and cross bones on the front of the hat shone in the torch light.

Abbie and Jack felt slightly uneasy.

'Well, where's your ship then?' demanded Jack again, trying to sound brave, even though he was beginning to feel a little nervous.

'Well, err… my ship,' the pirate went on thoughtfully, 'is err… coming soon to pick me up.'

Jack and Abbie felt more uneasy now. They wondered when the other pirates might arrive and would they be taken captive.

'What are you doing here?' asked Abbie.

'Well,' said the pirate, 'can I trust you two with my little secret?'

'Of course,' they replied, feeling rather intrigued and somewhat honoured that the pirate should trust them enough to confide in them his secret, having only just met them.

'Well, come a little closer and I shall tell you,' he beckoned.

Abbie drew the dinghy alongside the pirate and they climbed out. Jack tied the boat up to a rock near where the pirate was sitting.

They sat down on a rock ledge to the side of the pirate. There was bread and cheese and water and beer behind the rock, along with a blanket and a small wooden chest.

'You see, me kiddies,' the pirate started, 'I've been coming here for many years. In fact, far too many to remember,' he coughed slightly. 'This island, you see, Pearl Island, is a wonderful magical place. These waters are enchanted. Me and me pirate mates were sailing these waters, er… fishing,' he hesitated thoughtfully and then continued, 'when we spotted the most beautiful fish we ever saw. We spent many months trying to catch this fish and, one day, we did.'

'What, caught a fish?' Jack laughed. 'That's easy, I can catch loads of fish in a day.'

'Shush, Jack, let the pirate speak,' Abbie interrupted.

She was intrigued by the story but also aware the other pirates may arrive at any time.

'Ahh,' continued the pirate, 'you see, this fish was no ordinary fish. Oh no, no ordinary fish at all. It was beautiful. Its tail was the most beautiful turquoise you ever did see. It had beautiful golden hair and a face and body with arms and hands, can you believe that?' he asked, staring straight at the children.

'Well,' replied Abbie, even more interested than ever, 'it sounds like a mermaid but they are just made-up creatures and not real at all.'

'You see,' replied the pirate, 'that's what we thought, but this was real. A real live mermaid and she is called Lisel.'

The pirate went on to explain how after catching the mermaid the pirates didn't know what to do with her, so they decided to let her go back into the sea. The mermaid was so grateful to the pirates that she promised to bring them a bag of the finest pearls every year on the August full moon as a thank you for letting her go.

'So, you see, me kiddies, that's why I'm here, 'cos tonight's the full moon… er, I think, and my mermaid friend, Lisel, will come with the pearls.'

'I'm not sure it's a full moon tonight,' explained Abbie, who took an interest in stargazing and the moon. 'I think it's a full moon in a few days' time.'

The pirate went on to explain that he and his mates weren't exactly sure when the full moon was and he had, in fact, been in the cave, waiting for about a week already!

'Sometime soon she will come,' guessed the pirate. 'She always does.'

Jack and Abbie didn't quite know what to make of the pirate and his tale of the mermaid. Pirates don't exist now and mermaids certainly don't!

'What's your name?' Jack asked, feeling more at ease with the pirate now.

'Captain Pearly,' replied the pirate, 'and me shipmates are Crevettes and Mussels.'

'What, you've only got two mates on your pirate ship?' laughed Jack mockingly.

'Well, you see,' the pirate went on, 'it's not a big ship anymore. We've lost bits of her over the years, snagging her on rocks and rocky outcrops when the sea's been rough or we've fallen asleep. She's alright, though, still seaworthy. She patches up well.'

Abbie and Jack were really not sure what to make of Captain Pearly and his stories of mermaids and battered pirate ships, but neither could they understand what a dirty, scruffy man who looked a bit like a pirate would be doing living in a cave all on his own in the dark. How was he getting his food supplies, and getting in and out of the cave, and what was in that wooden chest?

Abbie looked at her watch in the torch light – they had been over an hour in the cave. She was unsure of the tides in these parts and there was a slight swell rising from the cooling breeze outside.

It was time for them to make their way back to the boat and join the family.

She knew they would be wondering where they were by now.

Abbie and Jack got up. 'Just before you go, what are your names?' enquired the pirate.

'I'm Jack and this is Abbie,' Jack replied.

'Well, pleased to meet you, me kiddies. Me and Mussels and Crevettes don't have many friends 'cos we're at sea most of the time. It's been a pleasure meeting you both.'

Captain Pearly rose to his feet and shook Jack and Abbie's hands.

'Well, it's been a pleasure meeting you too,' the children replied, and with that, they turned and made their way back to the dinghy.

The sun was still shining brightly and the cooling sea air smelt fresh and welcoming as the children emerged from the cave.

Jack and Abbie talked about their encounter with the pirate on their journey back to the yacht and decided they wouldn't tell anyone about it. It would be their secret. Captain Pearly seemed a nice enough chap, even though he was scruffy and dirty. The children felt it was an exciting adventure finding a pirate and hearing the stories of mermaids and pearls. No, there was definitely no need to share their adventure. After all, who would believe them?

The children enjoyed the rest of the day fishing off the boat with Grandad and catching sardines galore for tea.

Every now and then, Jack and Abbie couldn't help but look deep into the crystal-clear waters below, just to see if they might catch a glimpse of a mermaid tail, even though they knew that would be impossible.

The next day at breakfast, Nanny asked what the children would like to do today. It was sunny and hot, identical to all the other beautifully warm days they'd had so far.

'Sand castles,' said Bella, pointing to her bucket and spade on the deck.

'Yes, Bella and I want to play on the beach today, Nanny, please. We want to make sand castles and catch crabs,' Lola said, nodding in agreement.

'Okay, that sounds like a good idea,' Nanny replied.

'What about you two, what would you like to do?' Nanny asked, looking at Abbie and Jack.

'I'd like to go snorkelling,' said Abbie, looking at Jack.

'Yes, I would too,' replied Jack.

Abbie lent across and whispered in Jack's ear.

'We can go looking for pearls and mermaids,' she suggested.

Jack nodded in agreement.

'Well, that's settled then, we shall go to the beach today,' said Nanny. 'I'll get a picnic together and you can all get yourselves ready and gather up anything you want to take with you.'

The dinghy anchored just around the corner from where the yacht was moored.

It was a pretty little sandy cove. They set up camp on the beach with a delicious picnic that Nanny had made. Yummy sandwiches, sausages rolls, crisps and cakes, all their favourite things, with lots of fresh fruit and ice-cold drinks.

Abbie and Jack put on their snorkels and flippers.

'What are you hoping to see today?' Grandad asked.

'Don't really know,' Abbie replied, 'maybe some fish or shells.'

'Or a great big shark,' Jack laughed.

'Well, I hope not,' said Nanny. 'Sharks aren't around these waters, so you will be okay.'

Grandad laughed, 'Well, you never know, you may find a pearl. Keep your eyes open.'

Jack and Abbie looked at each other. They were secretly hoping they might catch a glimpse of the mermaid Captain Pearly had spoken about. This would become their secret mission while on holiday to try and see her. That is, if she existed.

Lola and Bella decided to take their bucket and nets and go over to the rocky pools to the side of where they were picnicking.

'Is the water warm in the pools?' Nanny asked as the children put their toes into the shallow waters.

'Yes, it's like a bath,' Lola replied, 'all lovely and warm.'

There were quite a few rocky pools, and Lola and Bella paddled amongst them, trying to catch the little fish that darted in and out of the rocky hollows and crevices.

The girls sat on the edge of a larger pool down nearer the water's edge. There were lots of interesting rocks covered in coloured seaweed that swayed to and fro with the movement of the water, gently rising and falling.

There were lots of pretty shells and, every now and then, a couple of small fish darted out from behind a rock and darted back again. After a while, Lola started to get bored.

'It's no good, Bella, we haven't caught any fish – only shells,' she complained.

Bella was busy studying the shimmering colours of the pearliest shells. The sunlight catching them, creating a rainbow of colour.

'Wow, that's beautiful!' exclaimed Lola excitedly.

Lola loved rainbows and shiny things. She had long blonde hair and was always brushing it.

'I wish I had a hairbrush that was rainbow coloured,' she said.

Bella had lost interest in the shells now and had started throwing them back into the pool, when she let out an excited yell.

'Fishes, fishes!' she cried, grabbing Lola by the arm and pulling her towards her.

'Look, Lola, big fishes.'

'Where?' asked Lola, looking deep into the water.

Through the rippling water, she could see deep down a face looking back up at her. She thought it was just her reflection in the water for a moment and then the face grew nearer and nearer.

Suddenly, with a splash of water, out popped the head and shoulders of a girl with long golden hair.

'Hello, are you a mermaid?' asked the girl with a smile.

Lola was startled for a moment. She wasn't sure what to make of what she was seeing. 'Err… no, I'm a girl called Lola,' she replied nervously.

'Oh,' replied the girl disappointedly.

'Is she a mermaid?' the girl continued, pointing at Bella.

'No, she's my cousin Bella and she's a girl too,' Lola answered.

'Mermaid, mermaid,' Bella joined in, repeating the new word she had just discovered.

'No, you're not a mermaid, Bella,' Lola said indignantly.

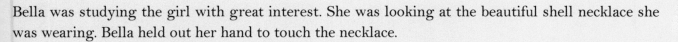

Bella was studying the girl with great interest. She was looking at the beautiful shell necklace she was wearing. Bella held out her hand to touch the necklace.

'Here, you can hold it if you want,' said the girl kindly and she untied the necklace and handed it to Bella.

'I thought you were a mermaid,' the girl said, turning to Lola.

'You look very much like me and I'm a mermaid.'

Lola looked puzzled. She had read about mermaids in books and even had a mermaid doll, but she didn't know they were real.

'Where's your tail then?' Lola asked.

With a swish and a splash, the mermaid propelled herself out of the water and on to the rock next to Lola.

'Wow, you really are a mermaid,' Lola gasped, staring at her beautiful tail.

'I've never seen a mermaid before,' Lola said.

'Can I touch your tail, please?' she asked.

'Yes, of course you can, but I am very ticklish,' the mermaid giggled.

'Wow!' exclaimed Lola. 'Your tail is beautiful and very soft.'

The mermaid laughed. She told Lola and Bella how she lived in the mermaid world under the sea and that they had a secret place above the sea in the centre of Pearl Island where they can bask and sunbathe in safety away from humans, and it's called Mermaid Bay.

'I love your long golden hair,' Lola admired, looking with interest at the mermaid's hair.

'I brush my hair a million times a day because I want long hair, just like yours. I have loads of hair clips too. Bella and I play hairdressers all the time.'

The mermaid looked puzzled. 'What's hairdressers?' she enquired.

'Oh, it's a shop you go to to have your hair cut or washed and dried or put into nice plaits and things,' Lola replied.

'That sounds wonderful,' sighed the mermaid.

'Shall I do your hair?' Lola asked the mermaid.

Lola loved any opportunity to do someone's hair.

The mermaid agreed with excitement.

Lola plaited the mermaid's hair and secured it at the end with one of the bands from her own hair. It was one of Lola's favourite Pony ones.

Bella had been busy studying the mermaid's necklace. She loved all the bright colours and shapes of the shells. Suddenly, the necklace fell from her grasp and descended deep into the pool.

'Don't worry,' said the mermaid, and with a swish of her tail, she was gone.

'Hello, girls,' said Nanny. 'What have you caught?'

'Nothing,' said Lola and Bella.

'We've been talking to a mermaid and she lives in the sea,' Lola went on.

'She's very pretty and I've done her hair for her.'

'Yes, mermaid fishes,' added Bella.

Nanny laughed. 'You are funny. Mermaids! Whatever next, you'll be telling me you've seen pirates, I expect. Come on, it's time we made our way back to the boat. We can play some games before supper.'

Abbie and Jack returned from their snorkelling trip around the cove without any luck of spotting mermaids. They saw many types of fish and sea creatures but unfortunately, no mermaids.

Later that evening when the children were settling down in bed, Lola told Jack and Abbie about their encounter with the mermaid earlier that day. Jack and Abbie could hardly believe their ears. Had they really seen the mermaid Captain Pearly had spoken about, the one they had gone looking for today? They decided Lola and Bella couldn't be trusted with their secret and they would never be believed by the adults, so it was best to say nothing to them about the pirate. It would be their secret, but now, they were thinking, just maybe... mermaids might exist after all.

The next day, Jack and Abbie decided to take the dinghy and explore more of the waters around the island.

The sea was calm and Grandad and Seb said it was okay to do so just for a couple of hours.

'Let's go and see the pirate first, shall we?' suggested Jack. 'We can tell him about Lola and Bella seeing the mermaid.'

'Good idea,' agreed Abbie.

Jack steered the dinghy across the water to the side of the headland and slowly approached the cave doorway. Abbie took control and manoeuvred the dinghy into the cave with skill. They tied the boat to a rock and carefully stepped out.

'Captain Pearly, are you there?' shouted Jack, his words echoing around the cave again and again and again until they faded.

'Cor blimey, no need to shout,' called out the pirate in his gruff voice.

'Is that you, Abbie and Jack?' he enquired.

'Yes, only us,' they replied in unison.

They walked along the rock path to where they could see the pirate sitting. A shaft of sunlight shone into the cave, lighting it up. It looked different from their visit before. The rocks shone and glistened and the crystals in the rocks twinkled like stars in the sunlight.

'Wow, the cave looks really pretty with all these twinkling diamonds!' exclaimed Abbie.

'Do you think they be diamonds?' enquired the pirate. 'I never thought of that before,' he said and removed his hat to scratch his head in a thoughtful way.

Captain Pearly was a kind chap but not very bright, the children had decided. For if they were real diamonds, they would have expected him to have found that out by now. They were, in fact, quartz crystals found in most of the rocks in these parts.

'We thought we'd call in and see you, as we have the dinghy for an hour or two,' Jack explained.

'That dinghy thing is very interesting,' replied the pirate, who had never been in anything with an outboard motor before.

'Would you like to come for a ride in it with us?' Abbie asked.

The pirate thought for a moment and then replied, 'Nah, couldn't possibly. I've got to wait for the full moon and I have to be here for it, don't want to miss the mermaid, you see.'

Jack and Abbie laughed. 'You won't miss it at the moment!' she exclaimed, 'It's still daytime outside and the full moon's at night. In fact, tonight is the full moon!' exclaimed Abbie, just realising that herself.

She went on to explain that he would be okay to come out in the boat for a little while, especially as it was still daytime.

'Okay,' agreed the pirate excitedly, 'this will be fun.'

They all climbed in the dinghy and Abbie carefully reversed it out of the cave.

The pirate was intrigued by the way the boat moved on its own with no sails and no wind, just a purring from the engine and froth of water spouting out the back.

Once out at sea, they headed away from the yacht. They didn't want anyone to see them with pirate Pearly on board.

'Where's your ship?' Jack asked the pirate.

'Ah, it's hidden in a cove that no one can see, 'Captain Pearly whispered, tapping the side of his nose.

This gesture, he explained to the children, meant it's a secret, a secret that only he and anyone he so wants to tell will know.

'Can we see it?' Jack asked.

Abbie was feeling slightly nervous at the thought of this idea.

''Course you can,' replied the pirate.

He showed the children the way ahead.

'It's just 'round the next rock.' Abbie guided the boat carefully through a maze of rocks ascending out of the sea.

'Me ship be 'round the next rock face,' the pirate informed them.

Slowly, in front of them, emerged pirate Pearly's ship.

'Wow!' exclaimed the children in surprise, 'It's, er… very old!'

Before them was a very old and somewhat battered ship.

'It looks like something from the medieval times,' Jack said.

'We've been doing the Mary Rose at school,' laughed Abbie.

It wasn't a big ship but it was wooden with a flat back and pointed front, with two mast poles, and at the top flew the Jolly Roger.

Pearly whistled a loud, shrill whistle in the direction of the ship.

'I bet those lazy good-for-nothings are asleep,' complained the pirate.

The dinghy made its way across the hidden bay, and the children realised they were completely surrounded by cliffs and rocks. It was a totally hidden bay within the island itself, only accessed across land or through the maze of rocks and cliffs the pirate had navigated them so carefully through.

Nearing the ship, they could see emerging from behind it a rather strange-looking raft with a blow-up inflatable chair attached. Sitting in the chair was a rather dirty, scruffy-looking man wearing a baseball cap. Attached to the raft and following behind was a lilo. There was another man lying on the lilo, only this time he was wearing a life vest and rubber ring.

'Coming, Captain, we're coming,' stuttered the man in the chair, rowing with a pair of oars as fast as he could.

'What are you doing, Crevette, you stupid pirate. Get back on board, you're not meant to leave the ship until you come to get me,' he insisted.

'Sorry, Captain, we thought you whistling was the signal for us to come and collect you,' Crevettes replied nervously.

'Well, it's not the full moon, is it? It's not dark, stupid,' the captain snapped, feeling rather proud of his new-found knowledge.

'No, 'course not,' stammered Crevettes, frantically changing course and paddling at speed back to where they had come from.

Following behind was the pirate on the lilo, who the children had decided must be Mussels.

Jack and Abbie looked at each other and raised their eyebrows. The captain's words seemed rather familiar. These pirates were the most unintelligent they could have imagined.

Once on board, the pirate captain introduced Abbie and Jack to Crevettes and Mussels. Names they had acquired from their parents after crustaceans of the sea. The same as Captain Pearly. He had acquired his name from sailing the waters around Pearl Island for many years and trading in pearls.

Trading in pearls had been forbidden by the government for a long time now, as the oysters that make them have been over-fished and their numbers declined. But Captain Pearly neither followed government orders, nor fished for oysters, he just collected his pearls once a year from the mermaid Lisel. They were the biggest and best you could find anywhere in the world.

'Is your raft safe?' Abbie enquired.

''Course it is,' replied the pirate. 'Never sinks, just floats across the water in all sea conditions.'

'But it's a blow-up chair and a lilo,' interrupted Jack.

'Oh, no, no, no, young Jack, these be treasures of the sea, you know. We find these treasures everywhere; we have cabins full of them.'

'Those aren't treasures,' Jack and Abbie laughed.

'What other treasures do you have then?' asked Abbie inquisitively.

The pirate took them below stairs and, sure enough, in all the cabins, there were pile after pile of lilos, caps, sunhats, bottles of sun lotion, towels, rubber rings, fishing nets, oars, life vests, costumes, surf boards, inflatables of every sort, goggles, snorkels, flip-flops and more things beside.

'These be the treasures of the sea alright,' said the pirate proudly.

'What do you do with them?' asked Jack

'We take them back to Parrot Islands and we sells them, that's what we do with them, young Jack.'

'Where's Parrot Islands?' Abbie asked inquisitively, for she had never heard of such a place and geography was one of her favourite subjects at school.

'About four months' sailing from here if the wind is right,' he answered, 'Sometimes five months. It depends if there's a lot of cloud in the sky, 'cos we follow the stars.'

'That be our home where all the pirates live now,' he continued. 'Been chased out of our old haunts and where we belonged but we likes Parrot Islands.'

'Wow!' exclaimed Abbie, 'You mean there's a special place that's full of pirates?'

'Well, I suppose so. You could say that. If you want to live the pirate ways, and I know nowt else,' the pirate continued. 'There be many pirates still at sea but don't follow the old ways no more.'

'Cor, real pirates still exist today, you mean?' asked Jack excitedly.

'Yep, all those that sails the seas be pirates.'

Jack and Abbie laughed. That couldn't possibly be so.

'What, Seb, our captain, is a pirate, are you saying?' the children laughed.

'Yep, if he be captain, he be pirate,' Captain Pearly replied dead seriously.

The children laughed even more. The thought of Seb being a pirate couldn't possibly be true, although they couldn't help but feel a small twinge of excitement at the thought.

'All who sail the seas be pirates, even those big white boats with lots of people on, they be pirates too,' the captain continued.

Abbie laughed, 'You mean cruise liners? The captains of cruise liners aren't pirates,' she giggled. 'They wear smart uniforms and speak very nicely, they definitely are not pirates,' she insisted.

The pirate laughed, 'You mark my words, young Abbie, all those who sail the seas be pirates. If they not living pirate ways now, then their fathers, grandfathers or great-grandfathers before them will have been pirates living the pirate ways. It's in the blood, you see. You can live on land but the sea calls you, it calls you back. So, somehow, if you have pirate blood, you will work at sea one day.'

The children listened with great interest. It sounded very convincing. Maybe, just maybe, there was some truth in what he was saying.

The captain went on, 'If a pirate knows he's a pirate, then there's one thing all pirates share.'

The children were engrossed.

'What's that?' they asked in awe.

'A gold tooth,' Captain Pearly whispered.

'All pirates who knows their past will have a gold tooth; it's a tradition passed down since forever. Look, here's mine.' And with that, the pirate opened his mouth and from the side of his gum shone a bright, shiny, solid gold tooth.

'And look,' he said, gesturing to Mussels and Crevettes to show the children their gold teeth.

The children were amazed and now even more convinced that Parrot Islands and pirates really do exist and maybe there were more pirates around than they ever knew.

'Can you tell us about Parrot Islands, please?' asked Abbie.

'Well,' started the pirate, 'it's our home and where pirates live. There are lots of 'em, little islands and parrots live on them. That's why most pirates have parrots.'

'Wow!' exclaimed Abbie. 'Imagine living on an island with beautiful parrots. They have such lovely colours.'

'Yep,' went on the pirate, 'and we are colourful too on Parrot Islands. We only wear our dark clothes when we sail the seas so as not to be seen, but when we're at home, we wear bright colours.'

'Really!' exclaimed Jack in disbelief.

'Yep,' the pirate replied, 'when we get back, we sell our treasures of the sea.'

'What, the lilos?' Jack butted in.

'Yep,' the pirate continued, 'the lilos and such like, they are sought after by our pirate friends. They make comfy mattresses and are fun to play on in the sea. We wear what we've found, so you see, we wear colourful things 'cos that's what we find floating in the sea. Here, Crevettes and Mussels will show you.'

In no time at all, the pirates appeared from a cabin full of treasures. Crevettes was wearing one green and one red flip-flop on each foot, bright-blue swimming shorts, a pink and white stripy tee shirt and a large cream floppy hat.

Next to him stood Mussels, wearing a black flipper on one foot and a brown sandal on the other, a knee-length yellow sundress, big red sunglasses and a bright-orange cap.

'You see,' said Captain Pearly proudly, 'these are our treasures of the sea and they are very sought after. Yep, we're a very colourful bunch back home.'

Abbie and Jack tried hard not to laugh. They had never seen anything so ridiculous. To think Parrot Islands was inhabited by colourful pirates wearing all sorts of mismatching clothing and furnishing their homes with inflatable furniture was just too much to take in and to imagine!

Abbie glanced at her watch.

'I think we ought to go now, Jack!' she exclaimed. 'We've been nearly two hours and they will start wondering where we are, back at the boat.'

With that, Captain Pearly and the children made their way back to the dinghy, waved farewell to Mussels and Crevettes and thanked them kindly for the fashion show.

Jack started the engine and, with the pirates' guidance, manoeuvred them carefully through the maze of rocks and cliffs out into the open sea and back to the cave.

'It's the full moon tonight,' Abbie reminded the captain. 'When do you expect the mermaid to arrive?'

'Dunno,' said the captain, 'but it's always when it's dark.'

The pirate climbed out of the dinghy and thanked the children for the ride.

'Will you be here tomorrow if we come?' Abbie enquired.

'Depends,' said the pirate. 'It depends when Mussels and Crevettes come and get me, and if they remember, they say they never hear my whistle!'

'What's in that chest?' Jack asked inquisitively.

'Ah, that be me map,' replied the pirate.

'A map?' said Jack. 'What sort of map?'

'Me treasure map, of course. Shows me where the treasure's buried. I brings it with me every time I come but I forgets to go looking for it! My great-grandfather buried a big chest here a long time ago.

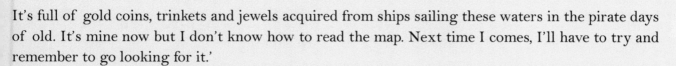

It's full of gold coins, trinkets and jewels acquired from ships sailing these waters in the pirate days of old. It's mine now but I don't know how to read the map. Next time I comes, I'll have to try and remember to go looking for it.'

'We can help you read the map,' Jack said with great excitement.

'Maybe tomorrow, Jack,' Abbie interrupted. 'The time is getting on and we must get back to the boat now.'

Jack agreed reluctantly but he knew Abbie was right, they must go back now. After all, there was always tomorrow.

'We'll come back tomorrow,' the children called back to the pirate, 'and help you read the map.'

'That be great, me kiddies,' replied the pirate as the dinghy disappeared through the entrance of the cave, turning right towards the boat.

Later that day, Nanny and Grandad and the children decided to spend some more time at the beach in the cove again.

Grandad, Abbie and Jack went over to the far side of the cove to do a spot of fishing. Nanny was hoping to cook fish for supper tonight if they were successful.

Nanny sat and looked at her crossword book.

Lola and Bella decided to wander over to the rock pools near where they had met the mermaid earlier.

'Stay where I can see you, please,' Nanny called out.

'We will,' Lola replied.

The girls climbed carefully over the rocks to the large rock pool they had been to before. The sea lapped the edge of the pool, causing a little spray of water to jump up in little pearl-like shapes.

'Bella, shall we call the mermaid and see if she's there?' Lola enquired excitedly.

Bella nodded her head. 'Mermaid,' she replied.

Lola cupped her hands around her mouth and whispered loudly, 'Mermaid, mermaid, are you there?'

The pool was empty.

'Mermaid, mermaid, are you there?' she whispered again.

The pool was empty and there was no sign of the mermaid this time.

'Hello, I'm over here, it's Lisel,' called a voice to the side of them. The mermaid appeared on a rock by the sea.

She leant forward, her arms crossed, and gently swished her tail up and down to the rhythm of the swaying water.

'Oh, there you are. You made me jump!' Lola said to the mermaid.

Bella turned her head towards the mermaid now.

'Mermaid, fishes,' she said.

The mermaid still had her hair in a plait secured with the Pony band Lola had done a couple of days ago.

'You're still wearing my hairband,' said Lola.

'Yes, I love it,' the mermaid replied. 'My friends love it too and think I am very lucky to have it. They also think I am very brave speaking to you.'

'Why are you brave talking to us?' enquired Lola.

'Because humans try to catch us,' replied the mermaid. 'So we stay away from you. I only spoke to you because I thought you were a mermaid,' she said.

The mermaid went on, 'But you were so kind to me that I know we can trust you and Bella.'

'Yes, you can' replied Lola. 'Me and Bella like you too,' Lola continued. 'Where do you live, Lisel?'

'Shall I show you?' she answered. 'I can take you there.'

'Oh, yes please, we'd love to come, wouldn't we, Bella?' Lola replied.

Bella nodded her head in agreement.

The mermaid flapped her tail and struck the water six times. Slowly, from the sea next to where the mermaid was sitting, a rock shape appeared, gently bobbing in the water. Slowly the rock moved onto the sand and stopped near the mermaid.

'Is that a turtle?' asked Lola.

'Yes. His name is Tommy and if you climb on his back, we can go to my secret cove where we mermaids live,' Lisel continued. 'It's not far, just through there.' And she pointed to a small opening in the rocks a few metres away.

'Come on, Bella, we can go just for a few minutes. Nanny won't miss us.' Lola glanced over to where Nanny was sitting. She was busy doing her crossword but glanced up to see the girls were okay. Nanny waved. Lola waved back.

'Oh,' sighed Lola. 'Nanny will miss us if we're not here.'

'Don't worry,' said the mermaid. 'Mermaids are enchanted because we don't fully exist in your world. This means enchanted time is no time at all, it's a mere blink of the eye. We can be there and back before your nanny knows you have gone. Do you believe me and trust me like I trust you?'

'Oh, well in that case, yes, we'll come. I do trust you, Lisel,' Lola replied.

Lola carefully placed one leg over the turtle's back and sat down.

'Come on, Bella, come to me. I'll help you,' Lola beckoned.

Bella held out her hand and Lola took it. She carefully guided Bella onto the turtle's back and helped her arrange her legs either side of Tommy's neck, as her legs were a little shorter than Lola's.

'Now, hold on tightly to Tommy's shell,' the mermaid guided.

The girls held on as tightly as they could and the turtle slowly slid back into the sea. Stirring his flippers slowly, they glided smoothly across the water with the sea gently rippling around their ankles.

In no time at all, they passed through the crack in the rock and emerged into a beautiful hidden cove.

All around them, sitting on rocks, were beautiful mermaids. Some were brushing their hair, some were making necklaces, some were looking at themselves in mirrors. All around them, the rocks sparkled like diamonds in the sunlight.

'This place is beautiful!' exclaimed Lola. 'It's like magic,' she continued. 'Those brushes and mirrors that your friends have are beautiful.'

'Yes, they are,' replied the mermaid. 'We make them ourselves from shells and our pets help us.'

'Your pets?' Lola enquired curiously.

'Yes, we have pets that make us beautiful white pearls that shine like moonlight and a delicate mother of pearl that sparkles and shines with all the colours of the rainbow. Our pets are called oysters and they live in their little houses in the water. We like looking after them and keeping them happy and safe here with us.'

Lola was amazed.

Bella pointed to the mermaids saying, 'Mermaid, fishes, mermaid, fishes, Tommy.' Tommy being another new word she had now learnt.

'Would you like to see my pet oyster, Lola?' the mermaid enquired excitedly.

'Definitely would,' Lola replied, and with that, Tommy made his way to the golden beach so the girls could climb off.

Lisel bobbed down under the water and, in a flash, popped up again. She had in her hand a bumpy shell that appeared from the outside to be rather dull and uninteresting.

She tapped the shell twice and it slowly opened, revealing a rainbow of colour and a shiny pearly ball inside.

'That's really pretty,' gasped Lola. She loved pretty things.

'That's a pearl,' the mermaid stated, pointing to the pearly ball sitting alongside the oyster.

'Our oyster pets make them for us and the mother of pearl too. That's how we make our pretty jewellery.'

'I wish I could have a pretty oyster like that,' Lola replied.

Bella reached out for the shell and Lisel passed it to her carefully.

'Be careful, Bella,' Lola commented. 'Don't drop it.'

'No,' said Bella. She loved all creatures, even wiggly worms.

Bella studied the shell and the oyster with great concentration.

'I'm sorry,' the mermaid began, 'but you can't have any oysters, as we protect and look after them. These pearls from my pet I give to my pirate friend.'

'You have a pirate friend?' Lola asked, feeling part excited and part nervous at the thought.

'Yes,' Lisel replied, 'but he's not bad, he's nice. He saved my life when I got captured once. I say thank you every year by giving him my best pearls.'

'Oh,' said Lola, not quite understanding fully the extent of what the mermaid had just said.

'But I have a present for you and for Bella too.'

The mermaid dived down into the sea and was gone.

Lola and Bella sat on the beach, admiring the beautiful mermaids. They had long hair of different colours and shades, some fair, some golden, some red and some dark.

Every one of them was beautiful, Lola thought, and to think Lisel thought Lola and Bella were mermaids, made Lola smile with delight and she flicked her long blonde hair, pretending to be a mermaid.

Lisel suddenly popped up in front of them and wriggled onto the beach a little way. She held out a pretty hairbrush to Lola. It was a rectangular shape with mother of pearl inlay all over it and edged with tiny shiny pearls.

'This is for you, Lola, from me to say thank you for being my friend, and even though you are not a mermaid, you look just like us.'

'Thank you,' gasped Lola. 'I will always look after this. Do you think it will make my hair grow?' she asked.

The mermaid laughed, 'Most definitely it will.'

Then the mermaid held out a pretty necklace for Bella. It was made with the prettiest shells she had ever seen and it was threaded together with fine strands of mermaid hair.

Lola took it from the mermaid and tied it around Bella's neck.

'Thank you, mermaid fishy,' Bella said and the mermaid laughed.

'It's time Tommy and I took you back to your rock pool now,' the mermaid suggested. 'Although enchanted time is no time at all, your family will miss you if we are away too long.'

Lola and Bella climbed onto Tommy's back and, holding on tightly, they all made their way across the bay and out through the opening to the open sea and across to the rock pool.

They could see Nanny looking at her crossword as they climbed off Tommy at the water's edge. Nanny looked up.

'Have you found anything interesting yet?' Nanny enquired.

'Yes, lots,' said Lola excitedly. 'And these are our friends, Nanny, Lisel and Tommy, and Lisel's a mermaid.'

Lola turned 'round to introduce them to Nanny, but they were gone, nowhere to be seen.

'You are funny, Lola,' Nanny laughed. 'Your imagination, Lola, is so funny.'

'But we have seen mermaids and we went for a ride on a turtle to Mermaid Bay. And look, we were given presents, look.'

Lola held out her hairbrush that Lisel had given her and she pointed to Bella's necklace. Bella took it off and handed it to Nanny so she could have a better look.

'They are beautiful!' exclaimed Nanny, 'Where did you find them?' she asked.

'We didn't find them, Nanny. The mermaid gave them to us,' Lola insisted.

'Well, they are lovely. I expect somebody must have left them here before we came.' Nanny went on, 'It would be a shame for the sea to take them, and they will be lost forever, so it will be okay for you take them with you,' Nanny said.

Soon, Grandad, Jack and Abbie returned from the far side of the beach with plenty of fish for tea.

'That's a pretty necklace, Bella,' Abbie noticed, admiring the pretty colours.

'Mm, fishes,' was Bella's reply.

Jack and Abbie laughed.

'Oh, the children found some things over by the rock pools,' Nanny said. 'I've said it will be okay to keep them, as no one is here to claim them. Besides, the tide will be in later and they will get swept out to sea. It will be a pity to lose them to the sea.'

The sun was beginning to go down and it was time to head back to the boat. The children had had an exciting day; first, Abbie and Jack had visited the pirate ship in Pirate Cove, and then Lola and Bella visited the mermaids in Mermaid Bay. They were all feeling rather tired and ready for their tea.

At bedtime, Lola removed the hairbrush from her pocket and started brushing her lovely long hair.

'What's that you've got there?' Jack asked.

'Oh, is that what you found on the beach today, Lola?' Abbie asked. 'Nanny told me you and Bella had found some things.'

'It's my special brush and no one else's,' Lola threatened.

'Alright,' said Jack. 'I was only asking!'

'Lisel the mermaid gave it to me and Bella got a necklace, but no one believes us anyway,' Lola grumbled.

Abbie and Jack looked at each other in surprise.

'What mermaid, Lola?' Jack asked gently, aware that Lola may get angry with him again.

'The mermaid I told you about before, but no one cares,' Lola replied, screwing her face up at Jack. 'She came to see us at the rock pool and we went to Mermaid Bay and rode on a turtle.'

Abbie and Jack looked at each other in astonishment. Maybe the mermaid did really exist after all. The hairbrush had pearls on it and pearls were what the pirate was here for.

'What did Nanny say when you were away for so long then?' Jack asked.

'Nanny didn't miss us,' Lola replied. 'It was a "blink of an eye time" the mermaid said,' Lola went on, 'and Bella's necklace is made with shells and mermaid hair, so there.'

Abbie looked out of the cabin window and saw the moon was up. It was a full moon and it shone like sunlight across the water. Jack joined Abbie at the window.

'Well, what do you make of that?' Jack asked Abbie.

'Well,' Abbie replied, 'I can't help but believe them, I think… look at what we did today with the pirate, I mean, and stories of Parrot Islands, and the mermaid's name being Lisel, the same as the pirate had said, and Lola hasn't met the pirate.'

'Yes,' agreed Jack, 'I think you're right. These waters must surely be enchanted after all.'

Jack and Abbie decided then and there that they would go back to see the pirate tomorrow as soon as they could and see if the mermaid had been.

Straight after breakfast, Abbie and Jack took the dinghy across the bay to the door of the cave. They carefully made their way inside.

'Are you there, Captain Pearly?' Jack called, but no answer came this time.

Abbie brought the boat to a halt and tied it to the rock.

Jack called out again and again, but there was no reply.

'He's gone,' Jack said, feeling quite sad. 'I'm going to miss him.'

'Me too,' added Abbie. 'I hope the mermaid came.'

'Look,' said Jack, shining his torch in the direction of where the pirate had sat.

There on the floor were two enormous pearls the size of marbles and a piece of paper.

The children climbed out of the boat and went over to the pearls.

Jack picked up the scrap of paper; it was what the bread had been wrapped in.

It was a note from the pirate. It merely said "jack Abbie".

'I think the mermaid did come, Jack,' Abbie said, 'and Captain Pearly has left these pearls for us.'

Jack agreed.

'We'll take them with us and treasure them,' Jack said.

'Yes, good idea,' agreed Abbie. 'We must ask Nanny and Grandad if we can come back here next year.'

The children climbed back into the dinghy and Jack shone his torch around the cave one last time. The quartz crystals in the rocks twinkled like millions of eyes looking at them.

'I shall miss him, you know, Abbie,' Jack said sadly. Abbie agreed.

The next day was their last day.

The children woke to the sun shining brightly through the curtains.

As Abbie looked out, she felt sad to think the holiday was over. They had all had a wonderful adventure and now it was to end.

Jack and Abbie looked at their giant pearls.

'This will remind me of Captain Pearly,' said Jack sadly.

'Yes,' agreed Abbie. 'And Crevettes and Mussels,' she giggled.

Jack joined in laughing and they giggled about the funny "treasures of the sea" and the inflatable furniture and Parrot Islands.

'We've had a great holiday, Abbie, haven't we?' Jack said. 'I really do hope we can come again next year.'

After breakfast, the family were ready to set sail.

'It will take us all day and all night to get home,' Grandad said.

With that, Seb started the engine and the anchor was raised.

'Next stop, England,' Nanny called.

Abbie and Jack stood with Seb and watched him guide the yacht back out to sea.

'Seb,' Abbie asked, 'do you believe in pirates and mermaids?'

Seb laughed. 'Well, some people talk about enchanted mermaids in these parts but I haven't seen one myself.'

'What about pirates, Seb? Have you seen any pirates?' Jack enquired.

'Pirates, you say?' said Seb. 'Well, pirates were around these parts many years ago but not anymore… well, so they say.' And he turned and smiled at the children, and as he smiled, the sunlight caught something at the side of his mouth and for a split second, there shone a glint of gold.

Jack and Abbie looked at each other in amazement.

'Did you see that?' Jack mouthed silently to Abbie.

Abbie nodded, her eyes and mouth wide open.

They both smiled at each other and tapped the side of their nose, just as Captain Pearly had done.

This was definitely their special secret.

Was Seb a pirate after all?

CPSIA information can be obtained
at www.ICGtesting.com
Printed in the USA
BVHW021101191119
564161BV00012BA/762/P

9 781528 915311